NATIVE AMERICAN ORAL HISTORIES

TRADITIONAL STORIES OF THE NORTHWEST COAST NATIONS

BY ANITA YASUDA

CONTENT CONSULTANT
Roger Fernandes
Storyteller
Lower Elwha Band of the S'Klallam Indians

Core Library

An Imprint of Abdo Publishing
abdopublishing.com

Cover image: A dancer in a raven mask performs at a potlatch.

abdopublishing.com

Published by Abdo Publishing, a division of ABDO, PO Box 398166, Minneapolis, Minnesota 55439. Copyright © 2018 by Abdo Consulting Group, Inc. International copyrights reserved in all countries. No part of this book may be reproduced in any form without written permission from the publisher. Core Library™ is a trademark and logo of Abdo Publishing.

Printed in the United States of America, North Mankato, Minnesota
032017
092017

Cover Photo: NativeStock
Interior Photos: NativeStock, 1; Werner Forman/Universal Images Group/Getty Images, 4–5, 31; Shutterstock Images, 7, 20–21, 45; Farah Nosh/Getty Images News/Getty Images, 8–9, 14–15, 36–37; Red Line Editorial, 10, 18; Philip A. Dwyer/Bellingham Herald/MCT/Tribune News Service/Getty Images, 23; Philip A. Dwyer/Bellingham Herald/AP Images, 25, 39; Wolfgang Kaehler/LightRocket/Getty Images, 28–29, 43

Editor: Arnold Ringstad
Imprint Designer: Maggie Villaume
Series Design Direction: Ryan Gale

Publisher's Cataloging-in-Publication Data

Names: Yasuda, Anita, author.
Title: Traditional stories of the Northwest Coast nations / by Anita Yasuda.
Description: Minneapolis, MN : Abdo Publishing, 2018. | Series: Native American
   oral histories | Includes bibliographical references and index.
Identifiers: LCCN 2016962134 | ISBN 9781532111747 (lib. bdg.) |
   ISBN 9781680789591 (ebook)
Subjects: LCSH: Indians of North America--Juvenile literature. | Indians of North
   America--Social life and customs--Juvenile literature. | Indian mythology--
   North America--Juvenile literature. | Indians of North America--Folklore--
   Juvenile literature.
Classification: DDC 979--dc23
   LC record available at http://lccn.loc.gov/2016962134

CONTENTS

NORTHWEST COAST STORYTELLERS

It is November in the village. The canoe paddles have been put away. Now the people in the big cedar house by the shore are coming together. Children, aunts, uncles, and grandparents gather under the house's roof. It is a time for sharing. Friends catch up on the news. As the sun rises, an elder signals a story is about to begin. Children lean forward. Will there be a journey to the sky? Will Raven play a trick? The story begins.

The longhouse has historically been an important meeting place for many Native American nations, including the Haida of the Northwest Coast.

THE NORTHWEST COAST AND ITS PEOPLE

The Northwest Coast presses against the Pacific Ocean to the west. It is more than 1,500 miles (2,400 km) long. The region begins in southern Alaska, a diverse land with many islands and fjords. The Northwest Coast's rocky shores sweep south into British Columbia, Washington, and Oregon. In these areas, the wild coast gives way to giant trees. There are stands of pine, fir, and cedar. The forest creeps west up the steep Coast and Cascade mountain ranges. Some of the peaks here reach more than 10,000 feet (3,000 m) high.

Native people have lived in the Northwest for thousands of years. More than 40 different Native tribes in at least five distinct cultural regions live along the coast and islands. Among the tribes are the Tlingit, Haida, Makah, and Chinook. The tribes are diverse in

The distinctive landscape of the Northwest Coast influenced the people that live there.

The Tlingit village of Kake sits on the Alaska coastline.

their geography, languages, and customs. However, these groups also share some elements of their cultures.

Traditionally, coastal nations lived in separate summer and winter villages. They set up their homes near the ocean or rivers. The waters became their food source. People fished in the ocean for halibut. They harvested prawns, crabs, and clams. Salmon was the most important fish. Tribes caught salmon in coastal and inland areas. Another important resource was the great cedar tree. Most tribes built wood-plank homes from

these trees. The Coast Salish built some of the largest houses. This tribal group included several smaller tribes, such as the Lummi. The Lummi call themselves Lhaq'temish, or "people of the sea." Their houses could be up to 120 feet (36 m) long.

THE SPOKEN WORD

As with all human cultures, stories have long been important to Northwest Coast peoples. They are a way for children to learn about the history and culture of

NORTHWEST COAST PEOPLES

This map shows the traditional locations of Northwest Coast Nations. What do you notice about the locations of the different tribes? How does the map help you understand the importance of the ocean to the cultures of the Pacific Northwest?

PACIFIC OCEAN

Tlingit

CANADA

Haida

British Columbia

'Namgis

Nuu-chah-nulth

Lummi

Upper Skagit

Makah

Squamish

Quileute

Hoh

Snohomish

Washington

Tulalip

Chinook

their tribe. Children learn these tales from parents, grandparents, elders, and leaders. Stories share values, morals, beliefs, philosophies, and wisdom. Each tribe has its own tales. There are a great variety of stories. The creation of the world is a common theme. There are stories of magical animals and of great heroes. Other tales focus on the environment. These tales are about the forest, mountains, streams, and ocean. They explain how the planet provides for the tribe.

Traditionally, stories were told only in the winter time. This was the season in which communities came together in longhouses. Stories helped people learn

CEDAR TREES

The cedar tree is especially important to the traditions of many Northwest Coast tribes. Some Native peoples wove its bark into clothing, hats, and blankets. Wood was also fashioned into tools. It became fishhooks, handles, and animal traps. Cedar is still used for totem poles and canoes. Artists may also craft it into boxes, bowls, or dishes.

about their role within the community. Some stories told them about life and death. Others explained the stars, the moon, or the seasons. Native cultures in the Northwest are still telling stories. Stories are a way for them to hear of their history. They are a way to entertain. Today, stories also serve another important purpose. As fewer people are able to speak Native languages, stories keep these languages alive.

PERSPECTIVES

VI HILBERT

Vi Hilbert was born in 1918. She was a tribal elder from Washington State. Her name in her own language was Taqseblu. She belonged to the Upper Skagit tribe. In Hilbert's family, people told stories and performed songs all year long. Her mother and father told her stories whenever she asked for one. She heard stories indoors, outdoors, and even in the car. Hilbert became a respected storyteller and teacher. She spent more than 40 years sharing her culture and language. She passed away in 2008.

STRAIGHT TO THE
SOURCE

Candace Weir-White is a Haida storyteller. She spoke about how Haida culture is being shared today:

> *It is an exciting time to be a young Haida person! . . .*
> *Each successive generation has . . . kept a spark of who we*
> *are alive and passed that on. . . . Each generation has been*
> *taking up a cause and moving us forward. Our generation*
> *will be remembered for what we do to revive our culture and*
> *remember our history. At this time, we have reclaimed our voice.*
> *We have our own museum and we interpret who we are and*
> *share what it means to be Haida with the world. We are tasked*
> *with the responsibility of not only learning and remembering*
> *all the songs, stories, and histories that are passed on to us but*
> *also with saving our language and our way of life and passing*
> *those on.*

Source: Cara Krmpotich and Laura Peers. *This Is Our Life: Haida Material Heritage and Changing Museum Practice.* Vancouver, Canada: UBC Press, 2014. Print. 166.

What's the Big Idea?
Take a close look at this passage. What is the main connection being made between oral traditions and culture? What can you tell about the importance of storytelling? Does it go beyond simply telling a story?

CREATING THE WORLD

In many traditional stories from Northwest Coast tribes, plants and animals have spirits. Raven is one of the most powerful spirits. In stories, Raven can change his shape. He may become a human child. Or he may change himself into a pine needle. In some traditions, Raven is mischievous. In other cultures, he is also seen as a teacher, a hero, and a guide. In one story, Raven steals the sun so the people will have light. The following is a Haida creation story. It shows how Raven created the world and then filled the land with trees.

A person dressed as Raven performs at the opening of a Haida heritage center in Canada.

THE STORY OF THE RAVEN

Long ago, there was only water and the sky. Raven flew and flew, but he could find no place to land. So he traveled into the sky country. Here he saw a row of homes. In one of the homes was the baby of the chief's daughter. Raven slid into the child's skin. But he became hungry and began eating the eyes of the villagers. So they let his cradle fall into the sea. When the Raven child climbed out, he was at the top of a totem pole.

RAVEN AND EAGLE

All Haida people are born into one of two social groups. They are the Raven and the Eagle. Membership is passed through the mother's line. People show which group they belong to through crests. A crest is an image that represents the group. A crest might be carved on a totem pole or sewn onto clothing.

Raven climbed down the pole. At the bottom, he met an old man. "Grandson," said the old man. "I have been waiting for you." The old man gave Raven two stones. One stone was black. The other stone was speckled. He told

Raven, "Bite a piece off each rock and spit them into the water."

Raven did as he was told. As Raven watched, the stones became trees. They grew larger until there was land. This is how the lands of the Haida came to be. Then Raven stole the sun from his grandfather. But Raven began to feel lonely. One day he saw tiny people hiding inside a clamshell. "Come out," called Raven. These people became the first Haida.

THE HAIDA LAND

According to the story, Raven split two stones. They became trees, which he then put in the water. One grew into the mainland and the other into the Haida's islands.

The original lands of the Haida people are a group of more than 150 islands. The islands are located off the coast of British Columbia. They are called Haida Gwaii, or "Islands of the People." Great cedar trees grow on the Haida Gwaii islands. The Raven story explains the

HAIDA
VILLAGES

This map of Haida Gwaii shows the locations of Haida villages as they existed when people from Canada and elsewhere visited the island in the 1800s. Why do you think the Haida chose to build their villages in these places? Think about how they might have traded with one another.

Kiusta

Yan

Masset

Kung

Hiellan

Kayung

PACIFIC OCEAN

N
W   E
S

Skidegate

Cha'atl

Cumshewa

Kaisun

Skedans

Tanu

Haida Gwaii

Skungwai (Ninstints)

source of these trees. It shows how central the cedar tree has been to Haida life.

THE HAIDA HOME

The Haida built their homes facing the water. As in the story, they arranged their homes in rows according to social rank. The higher a person's rank was, the closer he or she lived to the chief. Often, several families lived in the same house.

Some homes had totem poles near the front door. The Haida carved their poles from red cedar. A pole might have an oval hole cut into its base. This oval hole served as the door to the house. Other homes had a door next to the pole.

PERSPECTIVES
DU-KWI-BAXH

The Snohomish people of Washington State tell of Du-kwi-baxh. This is their name for the creator. Du-kwi-baxh prepared the world for people to come, creating a land of abundance. He gave each group of people a language. This is said to be why the Native peoples of Puget Sound speak so many different languages.

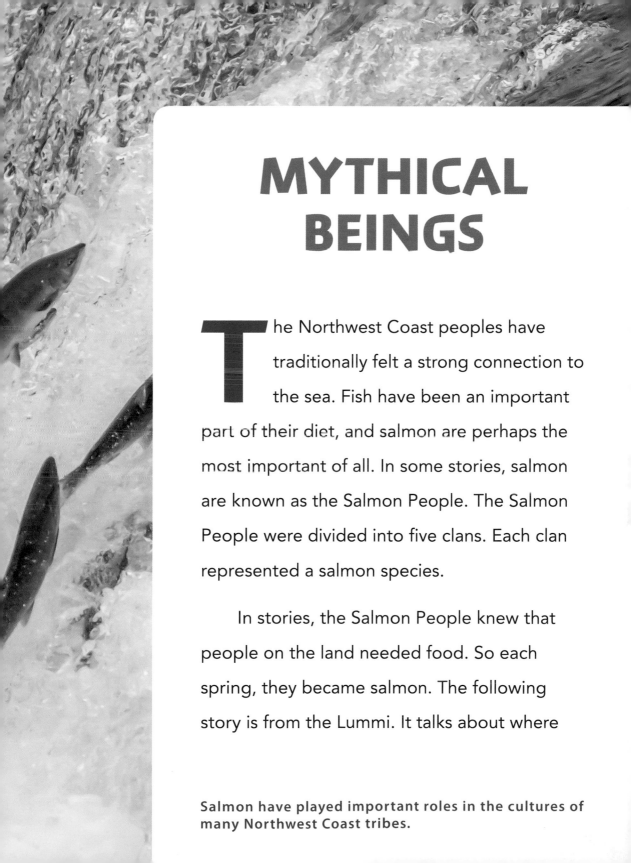

MYTHICAL BEINGS

The Northwest Coast peoples have traditionally felt a strong connection to the sea. Fish have been an important part of their diet, and salmon are perhaps the most important of all. In some stories, salmon are known as the Salmon People. The Salmon People were divided into five clans. Each clan represented a salmon species.

In stories, the Salmon People knew that people on the land needed food. So each spring, they became salmon. The following story is from the Lummi. It talks about where

Salmon have played important roles in the cultures of many Northwest Coast tribes.

SALMON SPECIES

There are five species of salmon on the West Coast. They are the Chinook, chum, coho, pink, and sockeye. After being born in freshwater streams, they spend most of their lives feeding in the ocean. They return to the stream of their birth to reproduce. Most sockeye salmon stay in the ocean for two to three years before returning home. In some years, millions of salmon return home. The fish jump and flop as they struggle against the current to make their way home.

salmon come from and how they should be treated.

THE SALMON WOMAN

There was a time when the people had little food to eat. They dug for roots. They drank tea made from berries. But this was not enough. Raven decided to find new food. He climbed into his favorite canoe.

Raven paddled until he became lost in a thick fog. He began to sing about his people. The Salmon Woman heard Raven's sad song. She turned into a human woman. Then she pretended to drown. She cried for

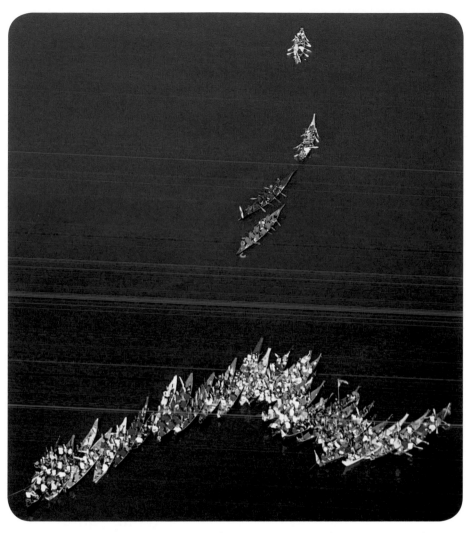

Canoes remain important to the Lummi people. A group of people in canoes gathered at a Lummi celebration in 2007.

help. Raven pulled her into the canoe and cared for her. Suddenly, the waters around the canoe filled with her children. All were different types of salmon. They were the Chinook, coho, sockeye, pink, and chum.

Then Salmon Woman sang, and the fog disappeared. Raven was able to find his way home.

When the people saw the salmon, they were happy. Soon, the smokehouse was full. But over time, the people stopped being grateful to Salmon Woman. So she sang a new song. As she sang, the dried and smoked salmon came back to life. They followed their mother into the water and left the village. The people were sorry for what they had done. After Raven had apologized to Salmon Woman, she agreed to bring her children back each year.

THE ARRIVAL OF THE SALMON

The story of the Salmon Woman shows the role of salmon in Lummi culture. Once, salmon was their most important food source. Coast tribes such as the Lummi explain the movement of the salmon through stories. As in the Salmon Woman story, salmon live in the ocean. Every year, they return in large groups to the streams where they were born. Once home, they lay

A teacher at a Lummi Nation school gives a student a hat at a salmon ceremony in 2012.

eggs and die. This is the salmon life cycle. This cycle traditionally shaped the lives of the Lummi people.

The Lummi moved to be near the salmon in the summer. Lummi men and women worked together to catch salmon. Women wove nettle fibers and willow into nets. Then, men hung the nets between two canoes. Today, the Lummi do not rely on the salmon as heavily as they once did. But they still fish and work to protect the salmon's habitat.

SQUAMISH FIRST NATIONS

The Squamish in British Columbia tell of four brothers who ask the Salmon People to come to their shores. Chief Spring Salmon invites the brothers to a feast. They are told to return the bones to the sea. But one brother keeps some of the bones. As a result, a salmon is missing its nose and cheeks. When the brother returns the bones, the salmon is restored. Chief Spring Salmon promises to visit the Squamish waters. But the bones of his people must be put back in the water each year.

FIRST SALMON CEREMONY

The story of the Salmon Woman is about respect. It teaches that animals play a role in keeping tribes alive. Storytellers felt it was important to acknowledge this role. Today, many tribes in the Northwest still show their thanks to the salmon. They hold a special feast. It is called the salmon ceremony.

Each tribe has its own traditions related to the salmon. Like the Lummi, the Tulalips are also a Coast Salish people. They begin their salmon ceremony with drumming and singing. The first salmon is brought to shore in a cedar canoe. After prayers are said, the salmon is cooked, and each person is given a piece. The bones of the salmon are then carried back to the river. Stories teach that the salmon will tell its people it was treated well.

FURTHER EVIDENCE

Chapter Three covers the importance of salmon to Northwest Coast tribes. What was one of the main points of this chapter? What key evidence supports this point? Find a quote on the website that supports the chapter's main point.

COLUMBIA RIVER INTER-TRIBAL FISH COMMISSION
abdocorelibrary.com/northwest-coast-nations

NATURAL PHENOMENA

People of the Northwest Coast tell tales of supernatural birds and sea mammals. Some of these stories explain natural events. The Thunderbird and the whale are popular characters. The Thunderbird is a giant bird that controls the weather. His flapping wings sound like thunder. Lightning flashes from his eyes.

Some stories call the Thunderbird the first whale hunter. These stories describe how he fought with a giant whale and made the ground shake. The following story draws on Hoh, Quileute, and Nuu-chah-nulth tales.

A depiction of the Thunderbird appears on a totem pole in a public park in Vancouver, British Columbia.

THE THUNDERBIRD
AND THE WHALE

Long ago, the people were hungry. The men could find no whales to hunt. They returned from the sea with empty canoes. There was no whale oil to drink. There was not even enough oil to dip their berries in. Thunderbird saw that the people were starving. He believed he could help. He quickly tucked a Lightning Snake beneath his wing. Then he left his home in the mountains for the ocean.

Thunderbird waited above the water. In time a great whale came to the surface. When it did, Thunderbird threw the Lightning Snake. The stunned whale could not dive below the waves. Thunderbird swooped down and grabbed it. Using all of his strength, Thunderbird lifted the whale. But he was forced to rest.

Each time Thunderbird set the whale down, a terrible battle broke out between him and the struggling whale. The ground rolled like waves. The sky darkened, lightning flashed, and thunder could be

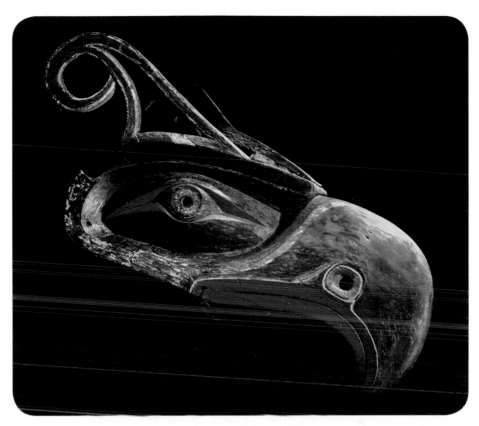

People of the Northwest Coast sometimes used Thunderbird masks or headdresses, such as this one from the Kwakwaka'wakw people, in ceremonies.

heard all around. Many times, the whale nearly escaped. But in the end, Thunderbird won. He gave the whale to the people. This is how the people had enough to eat.

WHALING

Many Northwest groups told of the Thunderbird and the whale. In this story, their battle may be describing an earthquake, a storm, or rough seas. The story highlights the importance of whales to many coastal cultures. Whales migrate along North America's West Coast. They became critical to cultures such as the Nuu-chah-nulth and Makah.

Men from these cultures used large canoes to hunt whales. Their canoes could be up to 40 feet (12 m) in length. Hunters believed that the whale gave its body to them. But the hunters had to prove they were worthy of the whale's great gift. They took part in rituals to prepare. They fasted before the hunt. They scrubbed their skin with shells until it bled.

THE POTLATCH

Whales were used for food and other goods. As the story explains, a single whale provided the Nuu-chah-nulth and Makah with large amounts of food. People harvested the meat and blubber. Whale oil was another important resource.

Some of the whale's meat and oil was traded to other tribes along the Northwest Coast. It was also given away through potlatches. A potlatch is a great gift-giving feast. The word *potlatch* comes from a Nuu-chah-nulth word meaning "to give."

Traditionally, the potlatch was held in the winter. A chief invited hundreds of guests. He would give out gifts to show his wealth and help the guests remember important announcements. These announcements could

PERSPECTIVES

THE THUNDERBIRD AND THE SEA MONSTER

The 'Namgis First Nation live on northern Vancouver Island. They believe that the Thunderbird is one of their ancestors. This belief is seen in one of their stories. Once, a sea monster changed himself into a man. He began to build a home, but he needed help. Nearby, he saw the Thunderbird sitting on a branch. "Help me, please," called the man to the Thunderbird. The Thunderbird used his strength to help the man. Then he too became a man.

TOTEM POLES

The totem pole is important to several cultures in the Northwest, including the Haida, Tlingit, and Nuu-chah-nulth. It serves different purposes in different cultures. In some of these societies, potlatches usually follow the raising of a new totem pole. The poles are carved with images important to a family's history. They may be carved with sacred objects or animal spirits, such as the Thunderbird. These animal spirits represent the crest of a family. A family has the right to use the crest because it believes an ancestor met with this spirit in the past.

be about marriages, agreements between families or tribes, a person taking on a new name, or other topics. Both Canada and the United States outlawed potlatches in the 1800s. In recent decades, potlatches have resumed. In the past, gifts included whale oil, canoes, or blankets. Today, these gifts might be clothing, flour, or coffee.

STRAIGHT TO THE
SOURCE

Charlotte Coté is a member of the Nuu-chah-nulth nation. Here she talks about the importance of whaling:

When I was a young girl, my grandfather, Hughie (Watts), would gather his grandchildren together and tell us stories that he had heard as a child. . . . There were those wonderful stories about Thunderbird and Whale, and the grand stories about our powerful . . . whalers. . . . Our whaling ancestors continue to breathe life into our rich whaling narratives, preserved and reinforced through oral traditions. They give power to our drums as we dance and support our voices as we sing. They continue to guide the hands of our artists as they create powerful images of the great Thunderbird and majestic Whale. We perform the ceremonies that keep us connected to and reaffirm our identities as whaling people.

Source: Charlotte Coté. *Spirits of Our Whaling Ancestors.* Seattle, WA: University of Washington Press, 2010. Print. 9.

Point of View

Why does Coté say whaling is an important part of Nuu-chah-nulth culture? Why is it a central theme in traditional stories from this region?

STORYTELLING TODAY

Native storytellers make their voices heard today. Some belong to Native storytelling groups. One such group is the Northwest Indian Storytellers Association (NISA). NISA aims to encourage the preservation of Native American culture and traditions. It hosts workshops and events open to the public. People gather at colleges and centers for storytelling festivals. At these events, NISA's artists present traditional stories.

Gene Tagaban is a member of NISA. He is a leading Tlingit storyteller. He shares stories he heard as a young child. Some of his stories are gathered from his life experiences.

Haida youths perform at an event on the Haida Gwaii.

He combines spoken word with dance and music to bring his stories to life. He also invites the audience to become part of the story. He may have children become characters. Or they may play instruments such as hand drums or rattles.

STORYTELLING IN SCHOOLS

In the late 1800s, the governments of the United States and Canada wanted to end Native culture. Native children were forced into government schools. These schools were abusive. Children were given new names, were told they could not speak their own languages, and received harsh punishments. Now, Native peoples keep their cultures strong. Some groups run their

Salmon is prepared at the salmon ceremony in Bellingham, Washington.

own schools. For example, the Lummi run a school in Bellingham, Washington. They hold their salmon ceremony at the school. The story of the Salmon Woman is a key part of the event. After the story is read, students sing in honor of the Salmon Woman.

The Haida also include their history and stories in their schools. Classes sometimes include books by Christie Harris. Harris was born in 1907. When she was a young girl, her family moved from the United States to British Columbia. She became interested in the culture of the Haida. As an adult, she wrote books

THE POWER OF STORYTELLING

Roger "Kawasa" Fernandes is a modern Coast Salish storyteller. He belongs to the Lower Elwha S'Klallam Tribe in Washington State. He does not believe stories should remain on the pages of a book. He believes they need to be told out loud. Only then, Fernandes says, will a story have meaning and power. He tells stories from his tribe and from other traditions. He also combines his presentations with music. Storytelling for Fernandes is a way to share and teach.

for children based on stories from Northwest Coast Native peoples. In the *Mouse Woman Trilogy*, Harris retells Haida stories.

STORYTELLING NOW

Storytelling on the Northwest Coast is exciting. Stories are not just for winter evenings. Each day, Native storytellers are sharing their rich cultures. They tell their stories out loud and write books. They appear at schools, theaters, state fairs, and festivals across North America. They reach even more people through television, film, radio, and the Internet.

Storytellers may share traditional stories. They tell stories with music, dance, and humor. These stories may describe the creation of the world, brave people, and supernatural beings. Or these artists may create new and original tales. Their stories tell what Native peoples are doing in modern times. As Native storytellers share their experiences, they preserve their cultures for future generations.

EXPLORE ONLINE

Chapter Five discusses modern storytellers and writers from Northwest Coast tribes. Go to the website listed below and watch the video about storyteller Ed Edmo. What new information did you learn from the video? What information was similar to Chapter Five?

STORYTELLER ED EDMO
abdocorelibrary.com/northwest-coast-nations

STORY
SUMMARIES

The Story of the Raven (Haida)

After climbing down a stone totem pole, Raven meets an old man. The old man gives Raven two special stones to drop in the water. The stones become cedar trees that then form land. This land becomes home to the Haida people. Later, Raven brings light to the world. He also frees the Haida people from a giant shell.

The Salmon Woman (Lummi)

While searching for food, Raven meets the Salmon Woman. She returns to his village with her children. The people have plenty of salmon to eat. However, when they stop being grateful, the Salmon Woman becomes sad and leaves with her children. After Raven apologizes, the Salmon Woman agrees to return each year.

The Thunderbird and the Whale (Hoh, Quileute, and Nuu-chah-nulth)

When the people are unable to capture a whale, the Thunderbird leaves his home in the mountains for the ocean to hunt for them. After the Thunderbird uses a Lightning

Snake to stun the whale, a great battle takes place. The
ground shakes, thunder booms, and lightning flashes
across the sky. The Thunderbird is victorious, and
he gives the whale to the people.

STOP AND
THINK

Tell the Tale

How might you retell one of the stories from this book in another format, such as a movie or a play? Describe how you would make the story come to life in this new format. How would your telling differ from the written version?

Dig Deeper

After reading this book, what questions do you still have about stories from the Northwest Coast Nations? With an adult's help, find a few reliable sources to answer your questions. Write a paragraph about what you have learned.

Take a Stand

Candace Weir-White thinks today is an exciting time for young people, as the Haida are actively sharing their culture. She talks about the responsibility of her people to learn and share their history, language, and culture. Do you think all young people would benefit from learning more about their history? Or do you think they should just concentrate on the future? Why?

Another View

This book talks about Nuu-chah-nulth and Makah whaling traditions. As you know, every source is different. Ask a librarian or another adult to help you find a new source about these traditions. Write a short essay comparing and contrasting the new source's point of view with that of this book's author. What is the point of view of each author? How are they similar and why? How are they different and why?

GLOSSARY

ancestors
the people a person is descended from

blubber
a layer of fat between the skin and muscle of whales

ceremony
a formal event

culture
the beliefs and customs of a particular group of people

fjord
a narrow, deep inlet of water, often between large cliffs

longhouse
a large rectangular home built from wood

migrate
when a group of animals moves from place to place

potlatch
a large gathering with feasting, singing, and dancing in which the host gives gifts

ritual
a ceremony that is performed in a certain way

sacred
something that is respected or believed to be holy

totem pole
a carved piece of wood that told a clan's or family's story

tribe
a group of Native people who share a common culture and language

LEARN
MORE

Books

Cuthbert, Megan, and Martha Jablonski-Jones. *Aboriginal Legends of Canada: Salish.* New York: Weigl, 2013.

Peratrovich, Roy A. *Little Whale: A Story of the Last Tlingit War Canoe.* Fairbanks: U of Alaska, 2016.

Spalding, Andrea, Darlene Gait, and Alfred Scow. *Secret of the Dance.* Victoria, BC: Orca Books, 2006.

Websites

To learn more about Native American Oral Histories, visit **abdobooklinks.com**. These links are routinely monitored and updated to provide the most current information available.

Visit **abdocorelibrary.com** for free additional tools for teachers and students.

INDEX

About the Author

Anita Yasuda is the author of more than 100 books for children. She enjoys writing biographies, books about science and social studies, and chapter books. Anita lives with her family in Huntington Beach, California, where you can find her on most days walking her dog along the shore.